BESSARABIAN STAMPS

Oleg Woolf

Translated by Boris Dralyuk

PHONEME
MEDIA
Los Angeles

BESSARABIAN STAMPS

ACKNOWLEDGEMENTS

Thank you to World Literature Today, Joyland, Bengal Lights, *and* Skidrow Penthouse. *I would like to thank Harold Abramowitz and Scott Arany for their scrupulous, sensitive work on the manuscript and layout. And I am especially grateful to David Shook, whose commitment to Oleg's work, my translation, and the cause of bringing world literature into English is rare and infinitely heartening.*

ISBN: 978-1939419286

Library of Congress Control Number: 2015932640

Cover painting by Alexander Telalim
Cover design by Jaya Nicely
Typeset by Scott Arany

Phoneme Media
1551 Colorado Blvd., Suite 201
Los Angeles, California 90041

Phoneme Media is a nonprofit publishing and film production house, a
fiscally sponsored project of Pen Center USA, dedicated to disseminating
and promoting literature in translation through books and film.

www.phonememedia.org

For Irina Mashinski

CONTENTS

TRANSLATOR'S PREFACE

"Three or four lines,
and you have the whole world"

Oleg Woolf's *Bessarabian Stamps* are just that—postage. Taken together, these humble, intricate little artifacts cover the charge of dispatching our imaginations to another world, posthaste. That world is the village of Sănduleni, one of those funny places that is neither here nor there, neither past nor present nor future. Yet somehow, against all odds, the mail is always delivered in "the dull hours between two at night and four in the morning."

My friend Oleg Woolf was born on December 3, 1954, in what is now the Republic of Moldova. He was raised in a border region, historically known as Bessarabia, peopled by ethnic Romanians, Turks, Slavs, and Jews, which has changed imperial hands more often than I can count. In many ways, his language— his entirely unique voice, his immediately recognizable inflection—was a product of this region, an outgrowth of this rich and troubled soil, like the "shoots of wild *bakon* grape vines, climbing roses, and ivy" he brings to life in "Brăndulescu and the Bulldozer." One can draw comparisons between his prose and other fruits of that soil, or soils much like it. The vibrant, vital microcosm of Sănduleni is reminiscent of Bruno Schulz's *Street of Crocodiles*, while Oleg's absurdist vision of the world—at once exuberant and tragic—calls to mind the Romanian masters Urmuz, Tristan Tzara, Eugène Ionesco, and Gellu Naum, as well as the Russian avant-gardists of the OBERIU, silenced by Stalin's terror.

Yet there is nothing quite like the *Bessarabian Stamps*—no destination as inviting and as beguiling as Sănduleni. There is a sincerity to Oleg's voice, a bittersweetness to his vision, that is all his own. His prose radiates a deep sense of generosity and humility that I have never encountered elsewhere, and I hope my translation brings that spirit across. This humility deserves special attention. Oleg's stories are stamps, not billboards or placards. They are supremely economical—prepared on "ant lard," as his character Ion Grigoreanu writes—but it is precisely this economy that lends them their power. So much is born of so little. Grigoreanu inscribes a book to his friend Dr. Petrike Munteanu with the following words: "May your reader's world be as economical as my writer's world." I am sure this is precisely what Oleg wishes for us: the ability to find riches where we least expect them, to see the world in a stamp.

I've tried to capture Oleg's gentle humor, his liberating paronomasia. Indeed, Oleg's *Stamps* are an homage to freedom, a freedom that ought to exist in every realm, but that one finds only in language—only "in the month of Oughtober, where the air is green with wood dust, and people cough in Russian, smiling firmly, so that one can't understand a thing, save for gar-ga-gar."

With warmth and irony, Oleg's stories explore what it means to live on the edges of empires that rise and fall, while Sănduleni abides. They teach us how to hold onto worlds so singular they cannot be allowed to disappear, how to preserve their fragile particularity. Oleg Woolf passed on July 21, 2011, but he has left us his *Stamps*— "And we'll put them in our back pocket, and we'll go on until the landscape alters beyond recognition. And on the corner, in the narrow half-light beneath the plum tree, we'll spot Feodasi, carefully reading and rereading an old book on the role of birds in Odessan seafaring."

Boris Dralyuk
Los Angeles, California, 2014

1.

Aurica and Van Gogh

ONE DAY A FREIGHT ARRIVED FROM GRIGORIOPOL WITH NO head car, but no one noticed. No one even noticed that no one noticed. People often pay no heed, at times, to things they later don't notice. No one, in fact, knows where this head car is—whether it arrived from Grigoriopol, whether it will arrive, whether there's even a railroad in those parts.

It was raining the kind of rain that exhortations can't help, and try as one might, one won't manage a thing against the water. Hello, there, said Feodasi, gazing at Grigoruţe from under his raincoat with that strange simultaneous gaze of his. His eyes were different hues of blue, and both looked off in one direction while his crooked nose pointed in another. Somehow, this physical discrepancy was met with no internal resistance, as if it dispelled the natural repulsiveness endemic to the residents of Sănduleni. Grigoruţe nodded. In the column marked "occupation," Feodasi was listed as a "village clairvoyant," as if it were possible to be an urban clairvoyant. Be that as it may, the document bearing the column lay in the nightstand of the rural elder Nike Podoleanu, who was famed for his homely grandiloquence.

Each time Grigoruțe's thoughts returned to this rain he would experience a profound sense of peace, a release from a certain presence of tragedy, a cramped zygote uniting loneliness with obscurity and death. It was as if the freight, having pulled into the final station—where everything speaks for itself, where one can't chime in with anything, where there's no one to exchange a word with—was firmly etched on his memory's smoke-stained back wall, which was already festooned with dented, sand-scrubbed aluminum kettles, old gloves, photographic portraits of sullen adolescents with youthfully athletic constitutions, and tin cups with rounded edges. And now the freight and all that detritus made up an internally consistent description of uniqueness, like those songs of the old Gypsy who left here for Paris right before the war and was handed over to the occupying authorities by a concierge he had known—because, in order to avoid pushing and shoving, a stab in the back is best administered by the one who stands nearest.

A conversation between a man and a woman is a conspiracy of rich men at midnight. Day begins with a man extending his hand to another man, and a woman—to another woman. This is why Grigoruțe first nodded silently, as if reconciled to the rain's demands, the continuance of life's concerns, and then said: Hello, there, Feodasi. You still alive, you old boot?

He heard no response over the din of the rain. The adolescent Mihai appeared and quickly passed by, peering into the darkness. At this time of year, adolescents experience a sense of captivity all their own, and their nights are long and poor in dreams. The chalice of possibilities was scraped so wholly empty by preceding generations that locals began life with a clean sheet, having barely enough time to inscribe it with the following: there is no harm in whatever amounts to less than pure evil. Everyone understood that the chicken one ate for lunch had no proper name, that the Sultan Abdülhamit ll, blessèd be his name, was a murid of the Shadhili Sheikh, and that whatever one does, sooner or later, is reflected in the balance of wrongs.

The train sighed and started off.

That same hour, in his office, Dr. Petrike Munteanu clambered up a ladder and pulled down one of the books that had been given him and remained unread. He opened it to the title page. "Dear friend," read the inscription in violet ink, "I gave you this book with the secret hope that you would never read it. Forgive me for the unsolicited gift, the secret thought, and the lordly inscription. A book is the worst possible gift—especially a book written in the 'literary' genre. Non-literary literature is a drawing at its most economical—prepared on the ant lard of a drawing. Three or four lines, and you have the whole world. May your reader's world be as economical as my writer's world. 1 am glad that you have gratefully limited yourself to this inscription. Yours, lon Grigoreanu."

Munteanu returned the book to the shelf and stood awhile on the ladder, glaring hatefully at the spine.

Hey, Petrike, there's trouble—open up, you goat, Grigoruțe suddenly cried from the street, at which point Feodasi frowned off to the side. Where they stood, near the old hospital built back in Turkish times, it was so dark that the rain stopped all at once, and the stars immediately clustered in tight formation. They burst, crunched, and crackled over Sănduleni, like a barrel of fermented cucumbers. Well, Petrike Munteanu cried back through the window with his velvety bass, at least write down my phone number by heart.

The Gypsy woman is dying, said Grigoruțe.

The three of them huddled in the oval of light beneath the bare bulb, which wobbled like an egg yolk at the bottom of a glass. Take me to the Pamirs, the Gypsy told them, pointing at the eastern wall, which at that moment sent down a shower of limestone. Death awaits at the Pamirs—clay death.

What they knew of the Gypsy was that she went by Asta, that she washed floorcloths till they were gleaming white for drying. No one visited her house, built by her great-grandfather on the side of town—and they avoided her by necessity, for she was well over a hundred, and remained a person of such openness, kindness, and strength that she was impossible to bear.

Aurica, the neighbor, came to pay her respects, and stood facing the window, sensing death with her back. She gazed with all her might at the stars, each of which swirled in a funnel. These stars were painted by the artist Van Gogh, but Aurica knew nothing of this, although her friend Gogeni[1] once visited from Georgia, where he lived with his parents and a cat named Sniff.

Then Aurica began to cry, and no one dared interfere, and she cried so long that, little by little, morning came, and Asta died, and there were no more gypsies in Sănduleni.

---

1   Gauguin, in Georgian.

II.

We Will Meet Winsmore in the Spring

SO MUCH SNOW FELL ON SĂNDULENI ON SAINT NICHOLAS Day that people silently dropped what they were doing, went out into the street, and watched. A month went by, and now a long wet sheet hovered behind the train on which Ion Sandu, a teacher of physics, was making his slow return from Kazan. It was spring. Approaching Donduşeni, confident that nothing else would occur, the teacher awoke on the upper berth with the amazement of a person who has just struck upon the theory of relativity. The window was spattered with wet snow. The wagon stood at the station square, and Sandu saw the local monument—a small block of marble hewn by a man who spent all his earnings on drink so long ago that a good many years have elapsed in the middling agedness of time.

Six months ago, Iliana bore Ion Sandu a first-born by the name of Winsmore, and the firstborn had entered the world so old that knowledgeable people, shaking their heads, tried to reassure her: nothing to it, they said, he'll fall right into childhood as he ages. And then she served them loaves and fishes, while her neighbor Žemania—whose cursing, like a snake bite, was deadliest when closest to the heart—uttered such nonsense that she spoiled her own mood. On the fingers of one hand, Žemania counted her husbands, insisting that the more lavish the wedding had been, the poorer the funeral. She wept silently, baring her soul, and Iliana consoled her as best she could. Mashenka, you may not understand many things, but you mustn't be a fool, Iliana, being of a different female gender, consoled Žemania, gazing into her unintentional face.

It was then that the snow fell on Saint Nicholas Day, and the habitual trees stood secure in the knowledge that the predicted had reliably occurred. The bountiful snow sped between them like the train by which Sandu will someday return from Kazan. We will meet Winsmore in the spring, Iliana thought off to the side, in the direction where Ion had vanished, and quiet gratitude settled in her heart—a self-sufficient, hardly self-aware gratitude to the first comer, as he switches on the headlights in the fog and rain, in the last quarter of his life, crossing obscure foothills at the beginning of a long winter.

A woman tries someone's manhood her whole life, brings it to its logical conclusion, and Sandu jumped off the train's highest steps, having spotted them right away—Iliana, little old Winsmore in his cucumber-colored jacket, and the very tiny dog Savka, the bridge of whose nose was, as usual, scrunched up. With one hand, Winsmore firmly gripped his mother's palm, with the other—a checkered canvas suitcase. He stared at his father, deep in thought, as if measuring him up for himself and the whole surrounding world. Hello, father, Winsmore would likely say, were he able to speak. You forgot this.

Film this year in your memory, Winsmore, and the reel would undoubtedly snap at this point, all glaring dazzlingly. White-eyed frames would shuffle past each other at random where, not long ago, living persons had acted and the lilac had bloomed. On one of these frames the black word "END" would arise and immediately disappear, and then a blinding light would blaze up in the theater—which is as cold and impatient as springtime on the wrong side of the tracks. And round-shouldered strangers would commence whistling through their fingers, demanding to have things their way, raging inappropriately, and hollering as if it were a bathhouse.

And so no one filmed them from above, nor even from the side—the angle from which we almost always look more alive. In fact, all this was so unreal that no one knows whether it was or wasn't real at all. The only argument in favor of its happening is us—meaning, nothing is impossible.

When you live with someone of the same blood, he betrays you in everything, Sandu told Iliana when these were the only things worth talking about. He is you yourself, save for a different gait.

Then they went to the cinema to see the evening show. They walked arm in arm, with the same gait, and watched the film all the way through. Their faces wore expressions so intimate that one could see almost nothing of the screen, and not a single reel broke, and the next day, they forgot the director's name.

III.

Mircea and Marica

CALL ME ALWAYS. VERY WELL, I'LL MAKE THE CALL ALWAYS. We'll always meet some other time. Today we'll meet someone else—Ionesco—you can hardly see him. He works, this Ionesco, with a specialization: village paramedic. Ever since he grew fat, he's lost a little weight, and when we meet him, he might tell us that the ailment's primary symptom is death—whether or not you work with a specialization. His relationship with death is very usual, very common; nothing about this relationship is unexpected, and it bears no relation to immortality or death. Many pity Ionesco, believing he has to earn his money on the side. The world is open to him, as if he were a blind man. This is exactly what the Georgian philosopher Gogeni told Aurica of Ionesco: unaccountably open, as if he were a blind man. This is why Ionesco will pass us by, having greeted us three times, because no matter what you do, what you think, tomorrow morning awaits you. There it sits, at the northern station, yawning, gaping, nose a-scraping. And in the morning, if we're lucky, we'll meet Gogeni himself. Last summer, the philosopher was around the same height, bald, and walked from the station just as now, and exclaimed just as now: ah, there you are! What a happy occasion, what luck, that we should meet on this sunny Sunday morning! If you remember this, do not forget the morning. Or best of all, remember nothing of this morning, and let it all remain as is. You ought to forget about our meeting altogether. In truth, we'd better never meet again.

And here is Aurica, here she comes, sunk in her walk, swept up in her Gypsy skirt. And no one will wear a skirt like Aurica Brăndulescu, no one will approach us and say: don't grieve, dodge with me awhile, free-wheeling drifters. Yesterday you went to fetch bread, matches, kerosene, tobacco, and wine, and now—you walk hatching plans. Take this medicinal ointment; apply it to your weeping wounds and burns until they heal on their own. Have some salt and some matches; go on, and put them in your back pocket.

And we'll put them in our back pocket, and we'll go on until the landscape alters beyond recognition. And on the corner, in the narrow half-light beneath the plum tree, we'll spot Feodasi, carefully reading and rereading an old book on the role of birds in Odessan seafaring.

So our day will begin, and we'll soon understand what sort of day it will be, though we may never learn how many of them are left, and why this ignorance helps people breathe so freely in the morning that they store it up, or tuck it behind their ears, like their last cigarette.

It isn't birds, you'll conclude. What role have they in seafaring? No, it's thoughts, plans, ideas, dreams— forgotten, unrealized by people. Perhaps this is so, I'll say. But still, I think there are things we'll never agree on, for there are two of us. You'll see it one way, I'll see it another. And vice versa. While together we'll know only the main things, about which there's almost nothing to know, really—as with truths familiar from childhood. For example, that there exists something quite similar to non-existence, and there's nowhere to run, no oven-door behind which one may disappear forever—and even if there were, then whatever might happen to us behind that door would still be happynows.

So, call me always, even twenty years from now. Let the former champions of their former trainers whisper, turning their whispering into ashes. Loneliness, death, death and loneliness—they still lack index numbers, the archers will tell the water polo players about us. They couldn't even bear to wait a little while longer; everything would have ended all by itself. You yourselves, they'll add one to another, you yourselves understand full well. Why, having picked up the hundred you dropped on the sidewalk, do you hide it in your sleeve? Doesn't it have something to do with your knocking off that bank in Fălești last week? And now all their thoughts turn to that business, and wherever they are, they've got common topics, common secrets. What is it to them that cinema is the liveliest of our motion picture arts? Will they ever make it in movies? They don't give two shakes about national pride, about glory—and it's all the same to them what they wear, so long as it's not too conspicuous. We'll have to answer, they say, to the full extent of the law. The state has precious few opportunities to engage the population. Precious few. Prison, military service, road construction, and nationality. For now, let's say, they're conspirators. This, no one can deny them. But that's for now. Let them blame the early snow, birds, Poles, social inspectors, autumn taxi drivers, and the whole unsubstantiated world. They're yawning, gaping, nose a-scraping. We'll see when we get there, they say, turning the corner, whirling their pedals.

Listen, you'll say about that bin behind the garage where we just tossed the garbage bags: let's wash our hands after the dump. And you'll make your way to the bathroom, to that old, flaking, threadbare towel that emits a barely visible light even during the day; and for a long time you'll carefully wipe your hands, daubing them with crumbs of fabric. I want to teach poetry and conspiracy. Don't go there, I'll answer. It may inspire a false sense of self-importance. Yes, you're right, Mircea,

I know this club and always forget that part of it. It's full of social inspectors, autumn taxi drivers, and financial movers and shakers.

In the evening, you leave the curtains half-drawn, so that, upon waking, we can lie awhile, quietly gazing at the morning foliage and the autumn sky. So that it's clear, cool, and quiet. So that, should the breeze pick up, the leaves might whip through the woods with the patter of falling rain. We'll put on our trench coats, walk out into the yard, and go on, not falling into conversation, until, on the corner, beneath the plum tree, we spot Feodasi with his book. And a small plane will fly overhead—the pilot's life in attachment.

IV.

Valia and Cantonist

CANTONIST LEFT THE MELANCHOLY DISTRICT CENTER, which lay besprinkled with solar dandruff, to put in his compulsory military service. One must admit that it was impulsive of his mother to cry: Off to the army, Cantonist! Let them make a trombone out of you!

Clearly, a person lives in the capacity of a second trombone, a senior engineer, a soldier, a beautiful woman, a machinist, a deputy director, a Sunday moviegoer. People won't drag themselves to hear a visiting lecturer on account of the terrible word "organoleptic," employed for a thing as indisputably necessary as wine tasting. Juvenile delinquents will beat the lecturer at a restaurant; they'll do it in such a way that his face will remain unmarked. Ex post facto, the privately sympathetic lieutenant-colonel Madden will develop a lively interest in whether the roast has or hasn't been served. There wasn't enough time, the lecturer will respond with painful, untimely insolence. Objectively speaking, we simply don't know what's worse for one's digestion, the lieutenant-colonel—who is so old that, to the lecturer, he seems completely drunk—will then note philosophically.

Being a discerning admirer of Immanuel Kant, nearing the girl of his dreams under the wise tutelage of his mother, Cantonist finally relinquished his rights to a self until granted special permission. Consequently, people in the hierarchy of military careerists—most of them deprived of a sense of humor and, hence, deprived of a sense of proportion—treated him with undisguised condescension. Suffering their secret beatings at night, during the days he awkwardly marched through the drill ground, the concrete map of which he will remember forever. One, two, and you'll find yourself a simple, bogus little trombone in the hierarchies of an undeniable, relentless lie, of which it is said: the state is a conspiracy of rich men procuring their own commodities under the name and title of the commonwealth.[2]

Cantonist's Sunday letters—which vividly painted tertiary, mundane scenes of garrison life—filled his mother's heart with vague suspicions. His mother stored the letters in a nameless pot, but when she realized the delight with which this epistolary ritual was censored in the unit's squalid office, she carried them off to the back yard.

---

2   Said by Thomas Moore.

Of the poor devils drudging in the vicinity, Cantonist knew that military friendship is based on shared misfortune, and disappears with the sun's first rays. Only love, and not friendship, based on shared misfortune has the right to life. As a matter of fact, that's what life is, thought Cantonist. Painfully, he became a trombone, grasping the futility and senselessness of evil. The endless suffering of evil, Cantonist mused, lies in the transience of weak and mortal creatures, who experience the insatiability of their imperfection vainly and without humiliation.

His inability to feel hatred, fear, and humiliation was offset by an acute sense of the absurd. Many years later, despite Kant's outstanding dissertation, this sense announced itself with the irrefutability of a military tattoo. Appearing on the body in the form of St. George slaying a small, clearly suffering dragon, this tattoo was the only argument in favor of the fact that Cantonist—whose boots squeaked obscurely in the snow while he stood guard over the station depots, staring at the thirty-year-old starry sky—and private Tsurkis—whose mind suddenly turned to the seventy billion sentient beings who had managed to die in the time it took this light to reach the retina of his eye—were one and the same person.

Being fifty years of age at the start of this narrative, he decided to grow out a beard; this wasn't based on the example set by people of his age and of his circle, but on the fact that, in his position, the quality of one's haircut and shave seemed inconsequential. His landlady, Valia, obviously concerned, asked why he no longer shaves. And why don't you, Cantonist asked for want of a better excuse. Because nothing grows, Valia replied with surprised laughter. And I—because something does, he snapped back.

Both had been tactlesss, smoothing over the inequality of their life experience, so that they were equal in the face of absurdity. Smiling, Cantonist thought that the tense estrangement with which she carelessly observed him should have been born of the hidden alienation of manhood, trying to seize what is intended for a child. Whatever he did or said with this beard appeared suspicious, like a drunken thief in a museum. What's that you've got there, he suddenly asked about a cup sitting atop the television. Bet yer from the have-beens..., said Valya. Yes, from the have-beens, the have-beens, said Cantonist. That's all of us here: from the have-beens. You too, you know, in all likelihood. Yes, said Valia, and you, which have-beens are you from—those, or these? On my great-grandfather's side, said Cantonist, we're all cantonists. It's a pity you're a cantonist, Misha, said Valia. I was told you were a philosopher. You don't say, said Cantonist. A pity, the landlady gently repeated. I've never seen a philosopher.

All the better, decided Cantonist, peering into her sweet, open face and mentally turning his own toward it. This is no excuse for non-acquaintance, not by a long shot. There's such a glut of people on this earth that tossing each other aside is an absolute crime.

V.

Ionesco and Feodasi

IONESCO ONCE PAID A VISIT TO FEODASI AND SAID: HELLO, Feodasi. You still alive, you old boot?

Feodasi heard these words, pursed his lips, and remained silent.

They lived alone, the two of them—Feodasi and his inner life. But very few besides Feodasi guessed as much. His inner life comprised all sorts of different things: trains, trees, clouds, the feelings Feodasi felt, the thoughts he thought—in general, all that was not Feodasi himself, but was instead his inner life. On account of his eyes, Feodasi was revered in Sănduleni as a soothsayer, interpreter, and miracle worker. So people often came to him for help, or just in case.

Of course, anyone who took it into their head to appeal to, and then come visit Feodasi immediately became a part of his inner world. Then Feodasi would look at them in amazement: where on earth did this one come from!

And so it happened this time, too. Feodasi first sat silent, then immediately asked Ionesco: And who do you happen to be? You wouldn't, by chance, be Ionesco, would you?

Hard to say, said Ionesco. Sometimes I think I'm a big, big bird, flying high beneath the clouds, and can see everything from up there. And other times, I'm just tiny Ionesco, and can see nothing but this Ionesco. But sometimes—and here Ionesco's eyes grew large and frightened—sometimes I can't even see this.

What? asked Feodasi.

Well, this one..., Ionesco then said with a small voice.

And what can you see? Feodasi asked grimly.

I can see nothing at all, Ionesco said in amazement. As though nothing existed—look as hard as you might. There's nothing in sight. Even the dark, you can't see. You can't even see that you can't see the dark.

Hmm, said Feodasi. Maybe you can, in fact, see just fine, but think that you can't. But then this is very strange. Because everyone in Sănduleni knows that they can see something, at least. Yet it may be that they can't see a thing, even their own darkness. So what, Ionesco, did you turn out to be different from everyone else? Or maybe you're not Ionesco at all, even?

These words seemed very unusual to Ionesco. Not even simply strange, but entirely extraordinary. As if someone suddenly spoke from an abandoned well on the edge of the village. He then looked at Feodasi a bit more closely, and suddenly saw that Feodasi—was not Feodasi, but a huge black bird with a thick, gray, chewed-up beak, sitting grimly with downcast eyes and turning its heavy wing, as if the wing cramped it. And it remained silent.

Who am I, then, if not Ionesco? Ionesco quietly asked the bird, or rather, asked Feodasi.

Could be anyone, Feodasi answered. He didn't so much answer, really—as simply say it. Whoever you are, would you like me to make some tea?

No, said Ionesco, we only drink tea when we're ill.

All right, farewell, then, Feodasi said, as if he weren't saying farewell. Don't fall ill.

All right, I won't, Ionesco responded.

And Feodasi's eyes followed him all the way to the corner, behind which the old, thick district road came rolling out. And Ionesco walked down the road a long time, until it got dark, and this made him feel warm, happy, and very ordinary.

VI.

Măriuţă and Iulian

AT ONE TIME FLORESCU SERVED IN THE ARCHITECTURAL Detachment. But then his immediate superior, Major Ivanishchenko, picked up Tourette's Syndrome—a disease that forces one to fire insults at people for no apparent reason. Water off a duck's back, of course—but in the Architectural Detachment, it's either fire or water all the time. So Florescu returned to Soroki, foregoing his severance pay, and married Măriuţă Dumbravă, who was like an apple orchard in a May thunderstorm.

She was born on the frigid, pitiless March wind and, fifteen and a half years later, left Iulian Florescu no choice. He wore a black mustache, lacked both severance pay and sense of humor, and exuded the charm of a serious man from nowhere—a charm she had never known before. And for this, Măriuţă Dumbravă punished him with her fatal beauty, which was more akin to fate than to the random bullet which shattered the Union's window and struck the water pitcher placed before her grandfather thirty years ago by a cloakroom attendant.

In point of fact, Florescu colored his mustache with henna, and his sense of humor was such that he never smiled at his own jokes. And so he wasn't really joking.

They say a sage has no fate, but the average person receives one along with a name. It turned out that Iulian Florescu sprouted and blossomed on Mǎriuţǎ Dumbravǎ in complete accordance with the surnames they'd inherited. If the Dumbravǎ means "forest glade" in Moldovan, then Florescu derives from the word "flower"—what else can one say?

This all happened so long ago that they've had time to rename the Architectural Detachment twice. Now they call it the Checkpoint Detachment, and a soft, crackled asphalt coats the little road to Fǎleşti with the easyness of an operatic bass. It was down this road that Florescu came to Ion Plǎcintǎ and, staring straight into his oily eyes, said: come out, 'ere, we've got to talk. What about? Plǎcintǎ asked wearily, tapping the doorjamb with an open palm. You know, Iulian said, and looked away.

When they finally released Iulian Florescu, he had just turned fifty-two, and looked all of sixty-five. His left foot was inked with the word "they're"—his right, with the word "tired." Both feet were tucked into Iulian's slippers, and he stood in a Moscow communal kitchen, staring through the gaping window—at this year's summer, at the playground, at the couple of old jalopies parked in the yard, and at his aunt Katinka, until she disappeared into the doorway, carrying her little case. It seemed to him that his whole bungling, bedraggled, crumpled life had turned into just this kind of case—old, just in case, and full of onion skins and holes, out of which a bottle of wine or a potato may come tumbling at any moment. His grief was such that he broke out laughing.

As fall approached, he was already in Chişinău. From there he rode out to Sănduleni along the district bus, and asked the first person he encountered for directions to moşu, Feodasi's house. What'd you mean, moşu? the man asked. A bunch of mishmash, you old mush. Then the man spat, shuffled his feet, lazily crossed the street, and said to Iulian: follow me.

Feodasi had no fate. His own father couldn't surmise the meaning of his mysterious name. As usual, Feodasi sat on a stool beneath a thick plum tree that was scored with elephantine wrinkles, and glanced disapprovingly at the 507th page of the fifth volume of Ivan Sigaev's work on Odessa seafaring. The stool was cobbled together by means of veneer by his great-grandfather, also named Feodasi. The great-grandfather dedicated the work to his great-grandson, swept up the woodchips, took the hammer and the remaining veneer back to the stables, dressed all in white, and willed his son not to bury the body in the village cemetery, but to burn it on a cherry wood pyre, scattering the ashes up the Dniester. Up, to the source, not down, he repeated. You got that? Yes, father, the son replied.

Our Feodasi was born a mere six months later. They say that a month after that, he entered the room where his family was having lunch, looked the petrified eaters over with great attention, and greeted them politely.

Iulian appeared in Feodasi's yard along with his guide. They found Feodasi beneath his tree, and the guide said: you still alive, you old boot? Feodasi pursed his lips, remained silent for a while, then asked, glancing at Florescu: you wouldn't, by chance, be Iulian? I would, Florescu responded. Where's your Măriuţă? asked Feodasi. She died, Florescu answered flatly.

They were silent for twenty minutes or so, listening as the cumulus clouds floated off toward the northwest with a whistle. The guide, too, floated off, whistling Shostakovich's "The Song of the Counterplan."

Then Florescu fell to his knees, and Feodasi said sharply: stand up, Florescu, you hear? Stand up!

And Iulian stood up.

Now they both stood tall, and Iulian stared at Feodasi as a conductor would stare into a tunnel. But, for some reason, he saw nothing—nothing save the stark naked Major Ivanishchenko, lying far, far away on the railroad ties and praying aloud for mercy. Iulian automatically picked up speed, then sharply decelerated and hit the brakes, but Major Ivanishchenko kept approaching faster and faster. Then Iulian pulled what he thought was the emergency brake and skidded to a stop, but something snapped, sparks flew, space tilted and, with a creak, began to curl up into a newspaper funnel, which was immediately filled with sunflower seeds. Then something like a rail tumbled onto Iulian's shoulder with a porcine squeal. His mother's face momentarily flashed before his eyes, and then his vision filled with a light so vivid that only the blind can see it. And, somewhere very close and somehow quite calmly, someone pronounced: well, that's it, Iulik. And it was the voice of Măriuţă Dumbravă.

Well, that's it, Iulian Florescu, said Feodasi, picking up the stool and placing it on one leg. Forgive me, in case. Head to Bălţi, stop by at 6 Owl Saints Street—they're tired of waiting for you.

VII.

Ursuleanu and the Window

IT STARTS WHEN URSULEANU NOTICED HE'D BEEN SLEEP-
ing with the window open. He lingered by the window
awhile, smoked three or four unfiltered cigarettes, and
then someone came by and silently fixed the telephone.
After that, Ursuleanu smoked three more cigarettes,
and then the phone began to ring. Ursuleanu picked
up. Open the window, said the phone in a tiny voice.
I've already opened it, said Ursuleanu. The receiver fell
silent, followed by rustling—and then, as if looking up
from some papers, a woman asked whether the window
was open. Have you opened the window yet? And you?
asked Ursuleanu. What? asked the woman. Yes, well, I,
said Ursuleanu. "Yes" what? the woman asked. Opened
it, said Ursuleanu. I don't understand, said the woman,
emphasizing "don't." It's difficult to make you out. You
say you've already done something, I don't understand
what. I said I've already opened it, Ursuleanu said with
no expression. Lord, said the woman, as if it were an
aside, where do they get these subscribers. You tell him
clearly: open the window, open the window. What are
you, deaf? Why are you shouting? I'm not shouting, said

Ursuleanu. Well, then, there's no need to shout, said the woman. Just go on, now, and open the window. I won't go, said Ursuleanu. What do you mean, you won't go? the woman replied in shock. Well, that does it. I tell him, go open the window, and he won't go. Where do these people come from? Go and open the window. Alright, Ursuleanu said, and remained silent for a bit. Have you opened the window? the woman asked sternly. Yes, I've opened it, Ursuleanu replied. Thank God, she said. Thank God. You can consider yourself lucky. You got off easy. You can live in peace.

Ursuleanu hung up and smoked two more cigarettes, one of them filtered. Then there was a knock at the door, and a young man donning the summertime uniform of an agricultural academy cadet appeared on the threshold. He barged right into the room, peeked under the nightstand, looked around, and said quietly: you know what? What? Ursuleanu asked, even more quietly. You can't lose with these people, said the cadet. Yes, not so much, Ursuleanu agreed. My grandfather served under Grigory Kotovsky, said the cadet, and wore a saber with his name etched into the blade. He and my grandmother quarreled on account of this saber when they were two hundred and fifty years old or so, put together. He went and chopped the wardrobe into little chips. Into fine dust, you can say. You won't tell anyone,

will you? What, me? Ursuleanu protested. Don't spread
it around, the cadet said gloomily. Grandma says to him:
what a fine thing to do, Syoma. I never liked that wardrobe. Frankly, I couldn't stand the thing. A certain Pole
left it to me—and this Pole was such a skirt-chaser, such
a ladies' man, he spent everything on drink, and lost
everything but that wardrobe. Sent his life up in flames,
God forgive me. Now everything is different. Thank
you, my dear, she says. Now that wardrobe is no more.
Now it'll no longer be an eyesore to us all. That's all.
Then they sat on the floor for a couple of years, the two
of them, hugging and crying. Have you got the window
open, here? Yes, actually, Ursuleanu replied. I understand, said the cadet. I'm off. If someone calls, tell them
you've had an inspection. Good night. Good night, said
Ursuleanu, smoked three cigarettes. At 10:16 the telephone rang again, but Ursuleanu didn't pick up. They
called again. Ursuleanu even wanted to pick up and say:
no one is home. But he didn't. You, he says, go ahead and
call. Dial up more often, or something. Everything will
shape up fine. Someone's sure to pick up, sooner or later.
Just keep your chin up. And don't hang up too soon.
Everything will fall into place, you'll see. That's how it
often happens, sometimes. Or just drop in, and pass it
along, only don't forget.

Ursuleanu closed the window, turned the latch, opened the transom, and went to sleep. Yet when he awoke, the window was once again open. He went to the window and glanced out at the street. But it was so quiet that there was no one out there.

VIII.

Ionesco and Brăndulescu

IONESCO LIVED ALONE. BUT HE WAS SO SMALL ONE COULD still barely see him.

One day he came to Brăndulescu, and Brăndulescu hardly noticed him. But Ionesco took no offense.

He simply said: greetings, Brăndulescu, I'm glad you're still alive. You're such an old goat, and still, nothing'll take you down. Know this: our world is predestined for death. It can't be helped.

Brăndulescu was very surprised to hear these words and said: who's there? I can't quite make anyone out.

And Ionesco responded: why, it's me, Ionesco. You can hardly see me, because I'm little old Ionesco—the other one isn't around. I'm alone. But what does it matter? Large or small—one or another. Life goes on, by and by, but death still turns out better.

Ah, well, Brăndulescu then said, sit down here, my friend. And he showed him to a chair. Have a glass of vin de masă, a few green onions. Let's drink at sunset for all the fine things you can't take with you. And if you do take them, they still remain.

Stay or go, it's all the same to us, now, Ionesco observed. We two grumblers are so old, we'll die soon, anyway, and won't be around any longer. Some kind of plague'll finish us off, in any case. Maybe even before the new year.

So what, said Brăndulescu, who, in fact, was really called Săndulenu. We'll croak, but our children will remain. And then our grandchildren, our great-grand-children will come of age. They'll all sit on this stool, here.

Yes, that's true, agreed Ionesco, who, in truth, was always called Ionescu. Only they'll croak someday, too. Some earlier, some later. One plague or another will lay them low. Even the great-grandchildren, they'll die, too. If, of course, they're ever born. And if they are born, they'll likely be sickly, and won't be long for this world. Or not very smart. The world is full of smart half-wits, Brăndulescu.

This is all very sad, said Brăndulescu and, with a smart expression, drank a bit, and took a few bites of a green onion, dipping it in salt each time. Very, very sad. So we should a raise a glass, so that they'll at least be happy. Because this happiness will someday end, too, so let it stay with them at least a little while. At least a couple of days.

Yes, said Ionesco, something's always ending. If it's not one thing, it's another. Some general case, it suddenly doesn't feel well—and then it's gone. You look, here it sits, and tomorrow it's gone entirely. Sometimes, it doesn't even make it till evening. It just barely had lunch, and come dinner time, there's no trace of it. They search for it, shout, it's already growing dark, and all in vain. As if it had never been.

Then Brăndulescu said: well, then, let's have a drink, while it's light out, to the fact that we have today. For this grapevine, at least. Or that little sun of ours.

Let's, agreed Ionesco, and even nodded. Still, none of this will last till the day after tomorrow. Or even tomorrow. Something will surely go wrong with it. But we can drink today. Tell me, is it true that you're called Săndulenu?

True, said Brăndulescu, taking a bite of the onion. My father's called Săndulenu, and my grandfather. And my great-grandfather, too.

So you're telling me you've got a great-grandfather in Sănduleni, too? Ionesco asked suspiciously.

Of course, I do, replied Brăndulescu, and sneezed.

You see, Ionesco remarked judiciously, you have a great-grandfather, and you're already sneezing. First thing you know, you'll croak. Isn't that sad?

It's very, very sad, Brăndulescu agreed and sneezed again.

What is this sneezing fit? Ionesco shouted hotbloodedly. It's almost time for me to go, and you're still sneezing. It's shameful to look at you.

Yes, yes, said Brăndulescu. It's very shameful.

At that point, Ionesco sprang from the stool, gloomy as a cloud, and went home. While Brăndulescu sat and sneezed. Probably on account of the onions. And then the rain came. Such rivers flowed, that you'd better watch.

Brăndulescu just watched and listened in silence to the rain, and it seemed that this rain would slowly transform into the murmur of some bygone voices, expired and empty. And suddenly he felt not so much sad, as somehow for nothing. He peered into the torrents of rain seriously and attentively—as if leaning over them—while they, in the usual manner of old men, forgetfully withdrew into themselves.

And then didn't even think, but simply felt something about his wife Aurica and wept, softly, like a cat.

IX.

Brăndulescu and the Bulldozer

SĂNDULENI HAD SUCH A FUTURE THAT, INSTEAD OF shelving it, the residents used it to heat their barns. Wanderers, casual passers-through—having borrowed some money and thrown their lots in together—would head to Sănduleni by foot and return home with a fiancee, or a pocketful of pumpkin seeds. They'd travel light, leaving straight from the market square, full of the future.

And there, on that square, stands a monument to (presumably) the Apostle Peter, who once visited this place. Strictly speaking, this is no monument; it is an ancient stone column, the contours of which suggest a human figure lifting its hands unto the heavens. According to legend, it is here that the Apostle, expounding in flawless Bessarabian, converted the pagans. They erected the monument a century later, building the city around it. His faith differed from that of the eparchy, and the church did not accept it, arguing that it was partially magic and witchcraft, and generally—apostasy and blasphemy.

The neighboring bishops cursed Sănduleni with anathemas, and one day, closer to evening, when Brăndulescu was busy trimming a vine, he heard the clink of bottles in the cellar. The earth swayed beneath his feet. There was such an uproar, he thought the roof had fallen in, and something unthinkable appeared before his eyes. A huge Caterpillar bulldozer, the color of sand, was moving across the market square in the direction of Peter and—Brăndulescu didn't have time enough to sit down, overcome by surprise—eclipsed everything around it. It was a blue hour, which precedes twilight in these places, and the bulldozer had reached the earliest stars. It was a mere ten feet from Peter, when it suddenly gave a great crack, a boom, a snap, and, lurching heavily, came to a standstill—so that one could hear the evening martins chirping against the crystal firmament over the river. Brăndulescu thought he had gone mad and died, and that the Apostle Peter himself would now approach him and place a hand on his shoulder, rattling his dense bunch of keys. For, like all courageous people Brăndulescu first died, then screwed up his inner eyes, and only set to work after that. He approached the bulldozer, climbed the ladder to the very top, peered into the cab, glanced around, whistled, and thoughtfully scratched his head.

The next day, a team of mechanics from the district's Technical Repair Station couldn't get the bulldozer to budge. Nothing changed the following day, either—and one of the mechanics said to another, younger mechanic: stop the machine.

The Caterpillar D9 model had previously been used by the Pentagon to clear minefields, and now it stood in front of Peter, like a worldly-wise pilgrim who came from a place to which the experienced do not return. This story later gave rise to speculation and rumors, and sometimes even to the most shameless lies. It soon took on the proportions of something rendered neither unto Caesar nor the archimandrite—the symbolism of a folk art rug, which one can examine indefinitely or not notice at all. This is why the rural elder Nike Podoleanu forbade people from picking the symbols apart for scrap metal. This is why the number of passers-through tripled, and why they themselves metamorphosed into elders and pilgrims, furtively relegating Sănduleni to somewhere "over there." On top of all this, it kept on raining such rains that one should really call it a season; five rains later, there appeared a lanky man of indeterminate age in a dazzling yellow jumpsuit. He stepped out of a UAZ truck, his long legs clad in army boots of brick-colored leather. He blew his nose into a handkerchief, looked at the sky, then at the bulldozer, now half-sunk into the fertile Bessarabian soil, and—judging by the expression on his face—said something stupid. Mint and young plantain sprang up from the Caterpillar tracks, and the armored cab was enveloped by shoots of wild *bakon* grape vines, climbing roses, and ivy.

Who's this McMahon? the elder Nike Podoleanu quietly asked, dialing the number (without capitals, we would remain alone, all by ourselves). It seems he is a man called that, came the reply from Chişinău.

The stranger lodged in a local one-star hotel, and, in the capacity of a neighbor, was invited to two funerals, attended three weddings (where it emerged that he was an American specialist in entangled affairs), and paid one visit to Feodasi. Then he vanished along with his boots, as inconspicuously as he had appeared. Another year passed and the Caterpillar D9 finally sank into the ground, leaving only the rusty sprout of its exhaust pipe sticking up in the air. For luck, local girls would place a wild rose or a bunch of lilacs in the pipe, while their in-laws would pour a full glass of young wine into it. Much later, when even the pipe disappeared, the engineer was accidentally identified by seasonal workers beneath the walls of the Orheiul Vechi monastery. His beard was tightly tucked into his trouser belt, and he responded to all questions with the clear (like autumn hazel) gaze of a wandering foreign specialist. This type is known, of course, to be deaf.

All this happened long, long ago, when guitar pins were tightened with the help of dining forks, and, as St. Silouan the Athonite put it, "that which was written with the Holy Spirit could only be read with the Holy Spirit." But just as before, the plums grew so large in Sănduleni that you wouldn't notice them, even if you circled around back of one.

The story of Brăndulescu and the bulldozer wasn't considered a lie, but a fabrication, and perhaps this is why people, with grave expressions, would listen to it all the way through.

We have almost nothing to add to this. After they blew up the monument to the Apostle Peter, a three-star hotel was built in its place. It stands empty, with the American Caterpillar D9 bulldozer in its foundation.

In the final analysis, the only worthwhile problem for man and the universe is what to do with oneself. Or what to do in one's own presence.

X.

Ileana and Sandu

ILEANA LIVED IN A VILLAGE WHOSE NAME SHE COULD barely remember. There's no shortage of villages where young women scrub a long floor, tucking up their skirts on the threshold of a new day. The village was common, like recollections fit for any weather—where everything happens anew, if one thinks about it seriously. All Ileana had to do was delve into her thoughts, and they would take the shape of sunspots at the very bottom of the ephedra growing on the outskirts of the village. Then they would form into viscid, unfamiliar, meaningful words, or lengthen into resonant, thin-walled music, which sends the soul straight to heaven. And then tears would well up all by themselves. Such were Ileana's thoughts. This is why she decided she couldn't think properly at all.

There was a serious mystery in these thoughts, entrusted to Ileana so that she could divide it in two, when the desire to reveal it turned to love. In the meantime, Ileana kept the mystery in her chest, beneath her heart, occasionally taking it out just to admire it—and at that moment, she had enough for everyone. She even had enough for the carpenter Theophanes, who often walked past her yard drunk, and who once took the neighbor's cat Manya by the head, struck the animal against the ground, and left it lying dead beside the gate. At that time, Ileana brought the mystery out to him in her sleep, carefully cradling it in her hands, in order to save him. At first he kept silent, shaking his curly head in shy wonderment and making eyes. Then he said: well, you think in the first place, and I in mine. After that, the neighbors got another cat, which went by another nickname, and Theophanes left the village and never came back. But Ileana still pitied both Manya and Theophanes, and once wept quietly in her sleep, seeing him dead in some unfamiliar town.

Once the village was flooded with such a light that only the blind can see it, having climbed to the very top on their smiles. The houses and trees no longer cast shadows, and the clouds lay so low that the pregnant dog Savka came out of her barn and commenced singing, while some passers-by crossed the street with their heads down, without even noticing.

This all happened so long ago that the road to Turkey went through Chernivtsi. Gazing out the window, the school physics teacher Ion Sandu saw an alley lined with linden trees, looking haggard in the light, like a railroad halt exhausted by passing trains. The instructor put on a pair of cream-colored boots, donned a green jacket, walked out of the house, slipped a piece of chocolate to a chubby tot counting pigeons by the fountain, and disappeared in a dubious-looking little clunker. So said an elderly passer-by, witnessing the incident. Well, yes, replied her friend. If you should meet a child, dig in your jacket pocket, see if you have a piece of candy or a ruble—and if you find something, give it. Suddenly, this child is yours, and you don't know it.

Ileana sat on the veranda behind her sewing machine, glancing out into the yard crammed with light, when someone knocked at the gate. She sat up and stared at the a focal point of light changing shape on the wall.

It's me, someone outside the gate cried tragically and fell silent. And this is me, thought Ileana, but had no time to respond. The gate swung open and a lanky young man with no trousers, a pair of cream-colored boots, and a cucumber-colored jacket appeared in the yard. Excuse me, the young man said sadly. You wouldn't happen to know what village this is, would you?

As if there are different villages.

Sănduleni, replied Ileana, in order to keep from laughing.

Yes, the young man said in surprise, actually, my name is Sandu. And you're Ileana, no? Yes, said Ileana.

And these are your pants. I'm just overlocking the inside seam. You wouldn't mind if I worked on it a couple minutes longer, would you? Of course I wouldn't mind, said Sandu. Especially since you overlock so masterfully. I should think so, said Ileana, my mother whipstitched these seams by hand. For my father. Times have changed now. Back then, you could get locked up for using machines—meant you were in business. That's true, Sandu agreed. Times are different now. Marry me. I will, said Ileana. Just let me finish this seam. Wait another minute, okay? Alright, said Sandu. I suppose I can wait another minute.

And he waited another minute, and then another year, until Ileana finished the seam and revealed her mystery.

But that is another Bessarabian stamp.

XI.

Petrov and Markov

AT THE KAZAN STATION, MARKOV OVERHEARD: RUSSIA IS for Russians. He turned and saw the rain, and beyond it—a little man with a narrow face, like an empty briefcase. The man stood on a bench. There was a smell of wet smoke. People were running. Markov, blinded by the train, greeted the little man with a gesture. That is, he simply waved his hand, remembering something from Tennyson: we Englishmen are, in fact, Celts, Saxons, and Danes. Or from Borges, who considered himself first and foremost a Basque, then a Spaniard, a Portuguese, an Englishman, and a Jew—because his family tree contained Acevedos and Pineiros, age-old Jewish-Portuguese families of Buenos Aires. Perhaps Russia is neither for Englishmen nor for Borges. And not for him, for Markov: it so happened that in the days of post-war sepia, his mother—nearly always at a separation's distance—loved a pardoned horse-thief from the ranks of the guitarists. Or maybe she didn't love him, maybe they called it something else back then. Maybe she couldn't live without him.

The train was set to arrive at 1:16, with a couple of minutes that one likes to hold in reserve. Strolling along the platform and whistling, a police officer named Petrov approached Markov with greetings from the dove on his left—and the brand new holster on his right. Markov dug a minutely checkered handkerchief from his pocket, went into a stall, stood there tugging at his nose, making eyes, and, for decency's sake, puffing out one of his old faces. He then quickly stepped into the train car departing for Udelnaya, where he had a meeting with Feodasi, and where Feodasi had a meeting with a certain Martemian. The angels on Martemian's shoulders—the black one and the white one—got mixed up, and so, in his fifty-second year, he went deaf in both ears. Or maybe not deaf. Maybe he just couldn't hear anything, such was his life.

There, over lunch, Ivan Markov learned that Martemian's people don't like America at all. This was stated bluntly and innocently, as one professes liking or disliking rice porridge, being able or unable to stand women. Of course, Martemian's people didn't know America, hadn't lived there, and this dislike could not constitute a strong feeling. It was rather a sort of permissible right, and that was clear to Markov; he inwardly agreed with their childish right to dislike, which had in it no righteousness of separation, but a kind of celebration of peaceful cash. At the very least, they knew Russia well enough to despise it. And this troubled him. Or didn't exactly trouble him, so much as seemed unpleasant—this is just too hard to figure out. It even appeared to him that they didn't like anyone at all.

The train was just approaching the platform, but one could already see the wet railway haul's sugary anthracite swishing out of the slits and slots. Returning in a stuffed car, Markov kept thinking about separation: that it has its own internal righteousness, which parting lacks. Separation is when you change the composition of your blood—and if you don't change it, then you become a displaced person living apart, saying things like, "I'm not well without you." In separation, you say nothing. Separation is when *I'm without you*. That's why separation is almost unthinkable. Possible, but not for everyone.

Barely recalling the haggard face of the missionary orator, he saw in it Ivan Markov, for whom every thought is only a preface to the next thought—who speaks with the kind of speed, confidence, and fervor fit, in his view, only for casting pearls. For Markov is an unfettered Gypsy scribe, who has penned two or three grandiose, abandoned volumes on love. These tomes are or aren't read, without love, by a social activist type—a sincere pawn in someone else's plan, which has far exceeded the pawn's expectations.

What will happen to this pawn, when conscientious people translate its ideals into their authority? Maybe nothing at all will happen, and stepping out at Kazan Station, Markov marched on, not glancing back at these thoughts of his, and not searching for yesterday's orator—as one searches for an old friend, whom it is customary to check against one's thoughts. He had just walked past the bench, when a titmouse perched on its back asked him: Why? Why?

The day was full of the kind of clouds one rarely sees in Moscow—sour cream-like, made of human souls. Shaggy Markov walked across the Bolshoy Kammeny Bridge, and each of the piers was more governmental than three railroad stations. Many of those he passed on the bridge may have read his books, but without love, grief, pleasure, separation, or regret, as one reads before bed: so as to fall sleep. So as to, just think, nine hundred pages—your eyes fall on any of them and the author says: you just read my thoughts. And me, what are his thoughts to me—they've just put me aside for a rainy day. You're a genius, too—go and brush your teeth. When did you ever see a genius brushing his teeth. They've never had teeth to begin with. They had gold ones put in when they were still children, so that they could pay for old age. Einstein, for instance—where did you see that he had teeth? They flew out of him with the speed of... Listen, stop jerking your legs. Remember Zina, married to Dr. Dwyer, everyone calls him Dier. First Zinaida comes in, then Dr. Dier's ears, one by one, then Dr. Dier himself, rubbing his ears together. Here he is in the dining room—small, nervous, with a huge sword, and his wearing his hereditary ears. Enough babbling. Go and wash your ears. It'll soon be dawn. I have to go to work, raise my children, you hear? Honor my parents and cleave to my wife. We've slept on it, and morning's morninger than evening. And the nails on my right hand now grow faster than those on my left. What are you doing, come on, I have to go to work soon, what is this nonsense you're talking about, close it from the other side. There's no other side.

Ivan Markov inhaled the faint Moscow air, was surprised by his lack of practice at living on Sundays, and walked on towards the Kiev Station.

Maybe this happened yesterday, and maybe it didn't happen at all—but it will certainly happen, or won't, as often happens with what hasn't yet happened. If it does happen, we will surely learn what's next.

XII.

Ileana and Mihai

ONE CLEAR JUNE MORNING THE RETIRED CIRCUS ARTIST Sîrbu's thoughts turned to his neighbor Ileana, whose husband was away teaching in Kazan for the third year.

If you think about something long enough, you may simply think it up altogether, and nothing remains aside from what you've thought up. And this is what happened then. Sîrbu, sighing, approached the window so as to admire the nameless architecture of the northern station's fortress, one of those sullen structures of which it is commonly said that it once stabled the horses of Count Vorontsov.

This all happened so long ago that even local snitches were forgiven for their frankness. Smoothing down his bushy chevelure upon meeting Ileana, Sîrbu would always congratulate her on the anniversary of Trafalgar. And happy Trafalgar Square Eve to you, as well, aren't you the lucky one, she would reply, smiling in such a way that Sîrbu thought: she is always smiling. Maybe she knew how to live. Not in the special sense often invested in those words, but simply to live. Not to die. Just to breathe. So, at least, it seemed to Sîrbu.

Then times grew not lean, exactly, but somehow disturbing. Villages began to elect people's representatives.

An old car's just fine, so long as it runs, Ileana, said Aurica, sitting at a table in the corner cafe, and Sîrbu gently pulled off his hat and placed it on his chest, bowing before them from his high window across the street.

None of the three voted, though the polling stations were stocked with young red wine—and next to two depleted ones, a half-empty bottle is as good as two full ones. It's not the *vox populi* that wins in life, but one's sympathies, Sîrbu yelled out the window. He was not heard. It was believed that Sîrbu received packages in the mail that were even more plywood than those in the old days. And on these packages, in big plywood ink letters, something like the following was inscribed: "Sichuan Gardebardenias of the Second Post-Type." People began to shun him, and even to avoid him entirely. Although there was no post in Sănduleni, but just a single mailbox.

But that's not why the girlfriends ignored his words. It was because they were looking at each other so intently, ad infinitum, that their heads began to spin—until they saw the vague contours of their fates emerge, like the corners of their lips in the darkness.

Ileana saw her old friend Aurica even less frequently than Aurica saw her, so profound was the look of absence they wore upon meeting. The cafe in Sănduleni is a place where there may be round tables (the restaurant is a place where they are unthinkable), and the friends sat at a round table in silence, not because they thus directed signs of inattention towards Sîrbu, but because everyone was equal to one another; no word, no action meant anything, even complete namesakes had different names; nothing would repeat—neither people, nor words, nor Sănduleni itself, where there never were any sequences, and where even between two trees one couldn't stretch a rope.

Oh, how wrong they were. Sănduleni had two railroad stations.

A chaos of curiosity lay behind both. But only behind the station called "western" did the lack of ambition make one invulnerable, did people go around hawking goods. The fields stretched out behind it, and beyond the fields lay a lake, in which there wasn't a drop of inspiration—which didn't refract the sun's rays. At a happy moment, Ileana recalled its clear, sunlit water. The lake needs no inspiration, she thought.

Freights arrived at the western station; as for the northern, we'll hardly touch on it, here. The boy Mihai, whose fate was just being decided in the world—where birds have grown so alienated from people that their names are the last things people learn in a foreign language—walked up to a freight at the western station and touched its buffer in the fog. This happened at the kind of summertime 3 a.m. when all you can do is think about everything all at once, touching a train's moist buffer. Above the lake, behind the railway smoke a smattering of stars arose and disappeared, independently inscribing the soundless problem of boyhood fate.

Perhaps the boy Mihai will someday remember all this about the western station, about the lake and the constellations, and how, carefully glancing around, he climbed into the car and lay down on the straw in the far corner, because the time had come. The car touched off almost immediately, and Mihai rode off almost immediately, and everything was suddenly lit with an inner light. And Mihai rode off in this light's bosom. He rode far, far away, all the way to Gangarsk, in the month of Oughtober, where the air is green with wood dust, and people cough in Russian, smiling firmly, so that one can't understand a thing, save for gar-ga-gar—and where they fell the old, reliable forest with the domestic Taiga chainsaw.

In Sănduleni and Bobyri, the universe was eternal, while in Bendyr and Lower Osman, it was mediated. This is why Sănduleni's universe could duplicate any of its realities with the squeak of an accountant's pen. It even duplicated itself whole—disdaining neither the invariance of entangled states, nor the stubbornness of its residents, nor the uniqueness of fates. This was not difficult: the sum of the confluence of circumstances was equal to the number of circumstances themselves, because they've both always existed, and none was arbitrary nor derivative, including that which we'd like to omit. After the end of the universe, which was accidentally divided by zero, it appeared in the doorway with varying degrees of probability, and this circumstance recurred relentlessly in all senses of probability, in all the splendor of the light's rainbows. Not surprisingly, in Sănduleni, where this narrative is fated to end more than once, people lived the same, ever-new life—constantly surrounded by crushed silk berries, silver willow, winter curse, and come-by-chance. But you just take a trip to Lower Osman, however, and everything changes all around, which is why it is impossible to find a street, a house, or even to gain a simple understanding of what is written above.

This is why Mihai, with a light heart, awoke at the northern station, on the most distant of side-tracks, where his car had been uncoupled.

But he never did understand what had happened.

XIII.

The Dancer of Malagura

ON THE DAY OF THE SUMMER SOLSTICE, IVAN MARKOV, an inpatient, sat on the veranda in a sports suit and sneakers, twirled a pen around his index finger, dropped it, picked it up and leaned over the table— above a piece of writing paper.

Dear brother, Markov wrote. Anyone who thinks he doesn't understand women is mistaken. He doesn't even see them.

Two days ago my lawyer was arguing her position, and I decided to look into her soul in all sincerity—but saw nothing there, except a long freight train receding into the autumnal landscape, and the landscape receding into the cloud cover.

Of course, there's nothing, the lawyer continued, nothing behind this, except a soft spot for trains and railroad tracks. Clearly, the defendant could not have hijacked the train, but even though his intent has been falsely interpreted, he deserves the minimum suspended sentence. For the man standing trial is of the suspended world (what man? asked the judge), located at the word, not at hand. The defendant is a Gypsy writer (what kind of a writer, d'you say?). He had neither a home, nor a profession—nothing, save for the railroad where he grew up.

It was a stretchable, leap year summer, brother, when, not surmising if the knowledge of your being dead or not is all the same to your God, you know nothing. Writing—which is the creation of community amid the unique, and not vice versa—was a matter of unnecessary and improper service, like bread and cheese where everyone's fed. The land, having survived the period which Georges Nivat beautifully labeled the "collapse of classical virtue," languished in abundance and simplicity.

The defendant committed no reprehensible acts, save for illegal ones, the prosecutor said. The lawyer nodded silently, looking off to the side, through the wide window, at the ancient crown of the sycamore, which spread its flayed hand of stripped branches.

When I was given my say, I stood up and declared that, as everyone knows, all things must pass, even though the mind is designed in such a way that it cannot grasp finality. That's why one seeks in a poem what is already present in a newborn's very first cry, and in prose, my brother—one seeks the remainder left when a man is divided by his death. For forty years I've lived in empty warehouses, on freight cars, on rear tracks, picking up this remainder.

It so happened, I said, that I recognized words before I recognized what are generally understood as their senses. Some of them, by that time, had already managed to show their true colors as scoundrels, others resembled their own shadows, the grandiloquence of the third kind would cling to my tongue like a rhyme, the fourth kind announced their resignation, the fifth were wintry, the sixth promenaded like tramps and triumphantly spat through a notch in their teeth. While every "lacerated wound" was a train made up of two flinching cars. The world was full of them, your honor: arrogant and fat, morose and cracked, fidgety and awkward. They kept the rhythm, settled into a second tempo and got their third breath, pulled on an old hat, embroidered on a tambour, and understood nothing of the senses imposed upon them—or rather, they understood nothing of their dreary half-criminal code which the unfortunate had to follow in daily life, at work, on the street, on the tram, and in the shop. A sense would tug its dependent word all the way to the fifth backyard of the tertiary signaling system, pulling it by the hand, gloomily chewing over the obvious: that isn't allowed, but this is. This situation dragged on, somewhat, and the true, intimate senses of certain words disclosed themselves to me when I was already rather mature in age. For instance, "let a thousand flowers bloom" turned its delightful flip side, and was now understood as nothing other than "let a hundred hairs fall out"—since Lao Tzu was always depicted fatally bald, as befits a Chinese sage, while there were plenty of flowers everywhere, regardless of him.

Now, being old, naive, and lame—sternly smacking my gums—I understand, your honor, that a person ages as his words lose weight, as they reveal their rigid carcass to the world, turning half-blind and inflexible, while their bones grow scales, coal, grief, weed, and lime. However, when I was a teenager hung about the alleys of Sănduleni, which were overgrown with words, these words needed no gardener, master, doctor, or writer. Literature was harmful to them, while a true creator, doffing his hat and scattering in apologies, was obliged to squeeze between them—hoping not to snag, tarnish, or damage them. The real talent wasn't the writer or the artist, but the whole world. The artist could only make a fool of a small part of the world with reverence, as an old mother makes a fool of a beauty with evening makeup.

Defendant, let's stick to the merits of the case, the judge said, her chair budging beneath her. Whose crying, what half-criminal code do you have in mind? What death are you talking about?

The quality of the object is the level of thought about it, replied the lawyer, making eyes at me. I object. The defendant is a drifter, a hobo king, a creative personality; he uses terminology that doesn't necessarily conform to the practice of jurisprudence. Like all of us, he deserves the right to fail.

Your honor, I said. Is it worth dragging out these proceedings? An old Gypsy in Malagura was so sleepy one evening that he sat up until midnight, thinking: well, so I'll lie down to sleep, and what will I then do at night. Damn it all to hell, he decided at last, and fell asleep watching the stars. This was a dangerous decision, your honor. For three hundred years, now, Malagura hasn't appeared on a single Gypsy map.

I ask the court to take that into account, the prosecutor said, muttering indignantly. We're now dealing with so-called Gypsy maps, which haven't been disclosed to the prosecution. What kinds of documents are these?

Enough, the judge said without expression and nodded in the stenographer's direction. May the record show that these words were not meant as a threat.

Brother, they have ordered that I be moved to a district rest house for the harmless, outside Moscow. This place reminds me, remotely, of the Kiev railway station in the capital, where, to a blockhead, everyone's an idiot.

And yet, if there's nothing else to say about a man, here they say he is capable. Or that he had an infectious laugh.

But the main thing one can say about him here is the most decisive—that women liked him. And that, nothing can beat. Because there's no one here that women like. One cannot love the resettlement of peoples, the speed of light in a vacuum. If you tell me that such people existed, and, when they died, they were mourned with the bitterest, most fatal womanly tears—well, then, they were liked by women. They won't return as Ivan Andreiches with thirteen volumes of *epistolae*, nor be re-dressed in memory, like a game animal, in any other way. But they might rise from the rain and snow in front of the trolley, oared by their beloved wife, Penelope, crying into her windshield: Annushka, here we are, come back to you, to your trolley, which rattles like a tumbling woodpile. Here we are before you, Sad Sacks at the saddest turn of Sadovy Street, turning our faces toward you, seeing you strewn with lilacs and sunlight.

And so, dear brother, if someone tells you that my prose reveals in the reader the feeling of loving and being loved—or, on the contrary, that it's difficult, incomprehensible, far-fetched, and indeterminate, tell them, with no doubt whatsoever, that women liked me, and that's the end of it. Say that I died every death that preceded me. Say that if you remain silent, dear brother, that means you're silent, sighing heavily and sadly. Tell them, after all, that there's a heat wave in the city, that geese and coast guard helicopters melt in flight, that fat policemen sleep with big sewed-on pockets full of honorific tokens. Everything sleeps. Little mustachioed lawyers sleep, having worked their tired nails free. Only your brother does not sleep, drinking tea of delicate petals made in faraway China. And a tired and crepuscular Gabriel appears before him, saying: what humble servant does not sleep here? Drinks tea of little petals? And your humble servant responds: this little mug of brewed tea is dear to me, hot and fragrant like a dancer from Malagura.

But Malagura is long gone, says Gabriel, Malagura is far away, and your dancer is dead. Her grave at the cemetery in Sănduleni is strewn with tea roses and brittle Gypsy lilac. Don't you know. I know, Markov says, but tell me, Archangel Gabriel, do I exist, or don't I? Dispel my doubts. You exist, Gabriel says, you are here, what's there to doubt? If that's the case, Markov says, then I have one desire. What need have you of desires, Gabriel asks sharply, what desire? Don't be clever with me. This isn't a desire, but a stamp, a mark, scar on the heart.

Yes, Markov says, it isn't a desire, but a stamp on the heart. But there are no Bessarabian stamps, since there's no post in Sănduleni, but just a single mailbox. That's why I called this stamp a desire. Much of what can be is not, and will never be, says Gabriel. So I will tell you. I'll help you, even if you're not in Sănduleni, and are not to return there. But remember: they'll call you a postal madman, a blasphemer, and a loner. Others will turn from you, as one turns from a rogue and impostor. Others will cross to the third, rear side of the street. While others, having turned from you, will hold you in contempt for losing, and will therefore hate you, Markov. It's only a step away from fear to contempt, but not even a step from contempt to hatred for the vanquished and the fallen. And then they'll speak of you harshly in a language whose every word will drag you into the gutter, betray you, and kill you. Will you be able to stand this? Markov. Will you accept it?

Yes, I'm ready, says Markov.

Well, then, says Gabriel.

I need a way out of entry zero into mine number ninety-nine.

Tell Arutiunov, was Gabriel's sole reply. I have to go. With these words, he crossed the courtyard and straddled a motorcycle, all dappled in sunny patches, started the engine, and puffed over the country road.

XIV.

Ionesco and the Hostess

THE HOSTESS ENTERED THE ROOM FROM ONE SIDE, WHILE
Ionesco entered it from the other, shaded side. In the
sunny room, in an earthenware bowl, bathed in blue
glaze, lay an apple with a singed quadrant. Approaching
it, the hostess grabbed it, threw it up in the air, caught it,
took a deafening bite, and disappeared behind a curtain,
while Ionesco touched the bowl.

There are things about which one would like to
form an opinion, he said toward the curtain.

Yeah, yeah, yeah, the hostess shot back.

Many things are symptomatic, said Ionesco, glancing after her. She made eyes at him in response, as if the
nature of these things existed, but was not such.

You're from Sănduleni? she asked declaratively.

From Sănduleni, said Ionesco. But it makes no dif-
ference. It's the same in its own way.

Go back home to Sănduleni while the buses still
run, said the hostess. Dumitru is due back in a week. I've
got a lot to do. No. 7 still runs.

No. 7, Ionesco specified.

It runs, said the hostess. But No. 99 is better still.

It'd be nice, said Ionesco.

Stepping out from behind the curtain, the hostess turned to the window frame. She looked out at the apple orchard, at bushes like drying sheets, at a rotted-out tree, at its decaying swarm of spiders and flies, at a squirrel in its sunny lashes.

Should I pass anything on? she asked.

Pass on that everything is bad and worthless.

Want an apple? the hostess said. Take a couple from the bushel in the yard.

She suddenly looked at Ionesco as if for the first time. He had come to visit Dumitru several times after he read his article in a journal, where the hostess worked as an editor. He hadn't managed to catch him a single time, and now sat in a chair in his inner navy coat, glaring at her inquiringly.

You see, it's like this..., said the hostess. You see, everything's a mistake.

I understand, said Ionesco, it's not all that simple.

Simple, not simple—truth that's yours, truth that's not yours, the hostess said intently. You, it seems, don't believe in God.

I'm not lettered, Ionesco said in a facial voice.

Is it possible not to believe in that which doesn't exist? said the hostess. Can one really not trust in it? Disbelieve in it?

In what? asked Ionesco.

In that which doesn't exist. Can one disbelieve in it?

A wasted effort, said Ionesco.

It follows, said the hostess, that you don't believe because He does exist.

Ionesco was surprised—not as an educated people, and just like that.

It looks like you've never been to the cemetery in Sănduleni, he said. You wouldn't happen to have a glass of little cabernet for the road?

They both walked up to the window, which was wet after the storm—to the apple orchard with its pillars of light. The neighbor's (it seems) boy shouted in full fervor: hey, rain, give me what you give the others, why dontcha!

Any village far exceeds the city in terms of events, but little happened in this one. More often that not, an event wouldn't happen—receding into a formal reply, becoming an event of dullness, of meager attendance. Longeurs, details were separated from the happenchaff along with the wheat. The locals walked over them—going as far into the sea as they could, up to the very last jump onto the last stone—from which one could see the whole sea all at once, the entire mass of the event. Waking this morning at a local hotel, Ionesco lay silently staring at the dull multitude of the sycamore outside the window. He weighed it on his synchronous internal balanscales. The outspokenness of the sycamore, its guttural words—which bore the mark of feelings expressed—had to be carried into the evening, so that one could then put one's hands on their warm plate, heated throughout the day. The workday was a bitter; he felt bitter about his life's work; the force of life had embittered him.

Ionesco turned to the hostess. She laughed myopically at the sun, like a typo. Everything gathered strength—the authority of beauty, the significance of expression. And he, Ionesco, had two faces—one was first, the other, second.

I'm off, then, said Ionesco. He descended the wooden steps; each bid him farewell with a squeak.

Farewell, said the hostess to his back. I'll pass it on.

XV

Thirteen Billion Years Since Speed-of-Light Day

PETREA BRUC WALKED UP TO THE FENCE, PEERED THROUGH a crack, and saw a bird. High-quality telescopes, said the bird, are made in the following manner: the bottom of a tin can, with a multitude of little holes, is inserted into a tube, followed by a light bulb. This allows one to economize on stars.

The milkman always drinks wine, said Bruc.

Come in, Petrike, said Feodasi.

Bruc prodded the wicket and walked in, although the gate was open. They were silent for about twenty minutes, listening to it drizzle on the road halfway to Kosauți.

It was so quiet that the elder Nike Podoleanu, heading to the village council along the same road, was stricken by an attack of light nausea. One could hear as women, who'd learned a week earlier of his return from London and, consequently, had trimmed their hair, whispered: wonder if he returned bearing good news?

Podoleanu turned into Basarab's yard, switched off the motor, stuck his head far out of the cabin, and either spat or asked some trifle. Well, said Bruc. I said how are you, said Podoleanu. By and by, killing time, Feodasi replied without a smile. Gather the people, Bruc, said Podoleanu.

They boarded for the night. The veranda faced the Dniester. It was one of those evenings that are always present in a person in the form of a landscape, overshadowed by events. A straight star hung above the house. A UAZ truck lit the veranda in passing, and the air behind it bayed at the moon. A train, that union of the living, chugged by in the distance.

Shooting glances back and forth, they set the table, placed the chairs close together, took their seats, each with his own dignity of expectation: valiant Brăndulescu, beaming Aurica, sighing like a school photo, the deaf American specialist in entangled states. Next to the American sat the ancient Georgian philosopher Gogeni, an old friend of the artist Van Gogh, who had painted the stars. Ion Sandu, the physics teacher, and his wife Ileana, beautiful, like hares that had leapt up and were suspended in pleasure, light as sparrows, whispered to one another ("So I see: he stands and talks in Latin, as if he could speak Latin ..."). Then entered the small, for a couple of minutes, Ionesco.

"Co-villagers and co-villagettes, from-theres and from-afars," said Podoleanu, lifting his glass so gently it was as if he were trying to estimate the length of its rim with his eye, and all turned their faces to him, as to a summertime rain in the city.

"We'll say farewell," Podoleanu said, and drank with such determination that the empty glass burst right on the table, and a girl named Efrosinia ran and immediately took it into the house.

A murmur spread around the table: "Tell us, elder, what you've got in mind"

"How do I know what I've got in mind," he replied. "There hasn't yet been a person in Sănduleni who'll say directly what's already clear, anyhow."

"Entry zero's somewhere around here, that's already clear," the girl Efrosinia suddenly said. "There have always been limestone boulders, here. The whole place is pitted with abandoned mine shafts. Two of them lead to a monastery. The other—zero speed. Everyone knows that."

"All in a land align along a line. That's all we know of the world and of ourselves," said the philosopher Gogeni.

Efrosinia spoke as if her legs dangled beneath her, but the murmuring at the table grew even worse—so that stripped sycamore in the yard, having absorbed strong views over the course of centuries, dumped part of these views onto the veranda.

When Efrosinia was born, she wasn't yet three years old. The town was small, but a lot of snow fell, and it was then that, for the first time, she not only saw, but recognized the snow and her tracks in it. Now, standing at the table, she caught sight of an infant gazing at her with serene hostility, and saw herself as an adult. She was overtaken by the sudden sense of irretrievability. Efrosinia and the child gazed at each other through an impenetrable thickness, forever forgotten and betrayed by one another. She ran round the table with a pitcher, filling glasses. Sandu and Ileana whispered to one another, sitting at the far end. The American slept, his head on the table. Others drank in silence, and when, finally, Podoleanu himself took a drink, everyone cast cautious, sidelong glances at his glass.

"We've got to go," said Podoleanu. "While it's dark."

They went. It wasn't far, and they traveled light, through a dubious grove—cut through with big reddish stars—the small ravine, the railroad embankment, toward the reader's train station, which almost didn't exist. And they went on, toward the plains that only opened up in the dark.

Everyone walked silently, pondering every step, until a light appeared in the final star on the edge of the village. It was then that Feodasi said: "Today is an anniversary: thirteen billion years since Speed-of-Light Day."

The author strolled along behind them, thinking of his own things. One could always tell by his jacket how long it had hung, rubbing against the wall of the little hotel, where it usually smells of prewar masonry, wet limestone plaster, and something else that the author conventionally defined as an "unmotivated, underivable idea." In point of fact, the smell is of the very bottom of realized stability, with a light admixture of cigarette smoke, kitchen-sink snitching, shoe polish (black), long-standing grudge, and petty betrayal. But the author didn't know about this yet, and constantly riffled through his jacket pockets in search of either cigarettes, or an unchangeable gold ducat—recalling, with bitterness and admiration, the Gypsy Asta: is she searching for them, groping for them, as for that unchangeable gold ducat, which, if you clasp it between your teeth, will forever cure you of old age, infirmity, pride, and desolation. How meager is our knowledge of one another. How rich we are in our imaginings about the snake vinegar of life in general. How sparingly each of us wields his narrow power. So thought the author, recalling the Gypsy Asta, standing at the crossroads amid his not-too-distant, gloomy kinfolk. Isn't that Asta, waving at them with one hand and adjusting her unruly spyglass with the other—glancing, as usual, either at the brittle Gypsy lilac, or into the imploding nowhere. No, he was mistaken.

The author saw them off one by one. First, Feodasi, behind whom, as usual, straggled the boy Mihai, toting the older man's tobacco pouch and pipe. Then, Brăndulescu. After him, the bearded American in a brick-colored, semi-military boot. The last thing the author managed to sight in the dark abandoned mine shaft was the face of Ileana, who had just then turned toward the stars that bathed it in light. When we meet again, it'll be light as can be, it seems, is what she said.

XVI.

Mailmen and Bicyclists

ON THE OUTSKIRTS OF THE VILLAGE STOOD A BOX WITH the following inscription: to the archangel Gabriel. It was painted blue and stood on legs that had been dug in, most likely, with a garden knife rather than a shovel.

In the dull hours between two at night and four in the morning, a bicyclist would ride up to the box and collect the mail.

OLEG WOOLF was born in 1954 in Moldova and passed away in 2011 in the United States. A physicist by training, he spent a number of years on geophysical expeditions throughout the former  Soviet Union. His poems and prose have appeared in many leading literary journals in Russia and abroad since the 1990s. Along with his wife, Irina Mashinski, he was the founder and editor of the bilingual press StoSvet and its journal, *Cardinal Points*.

BORIS DRALYUK has translated and co-translated several volumes of poetry and prose from Russian and Polish, and is co-editor, with Robert Chandler and Irina Mashinski, of the  forthcoming *Penguin Book of Russian Poetry*.

www.phonememedia.org

CPSIA information can be obtained at www.ICGtesting.com
Printed in the USA
LVOW12s2314130215

426972LV00003B/8/P